Seeds, Weeds and Spaghetti Trees

Cally Gee

CWR

Editing, design and production by CWR.
Cover image: Cally Gee and CWR
Printed in the UK by Linney
ISBN: 978-1-78259-940-1

PRINTED MARCH 2019

This book is dedicated to my Grannie and Grandpa, who loved their vegetable patch and garden.

They left a legacy of generous hospitality and love, and I am deeply grateful and honoured to have been their granddaughter.

I would like to acknowledge the extent of generosity and hospitality shared with me during the creation of this book. I could not have accomplished it without a long list of kind supporters. Your pets, vegetable patches, sheds and homes have brought me so much joy – my sincere thanks.

Miniphant would like to thank all the children that helped him imagine baked bean plants and spaghetti trees. 'Thank you for sharing your wonderful ideas in brilliant pictures. I liked them very much. Love Miniphant x'

Dear Mini Friend,

Hello! Welcome to another **Miniphant & Me** book.

My friends and I are so excited to share our adventures with you!

Our stories talk about:

thoughts in our head...

feelings in our heart...

and actions with our body...

because the way we *think* changes the way we *feel* and what we choose to do.

See if you can spot these in the story!

Learning how to share with others is an important part of growing up. Being pleased when someone else is happy shows how grown up we can be. It's not always easy; sometimes we stop sharing and start comparing. We might decide to do something unkind because we are feeling jealous.

The vegetable patch in today's story was a wonderful place for me to learn how to turn my 'jealous' weeds into 'joy-filled' seeds, and you'll see how my friends, Mole and Robin, do some sharing of their own too.

At the back of the book you will find some Bedtime Thoughts and Daytime Fun activities to do. There are also extra fun things for you to do on my special website! I'll tell you more about them at the end of the story.

Love, **Miniphant** x

One last thing to look out for: carrots get pulled up everywhere in the story! Can you find them?

Miniphant woke up to the sound of dirt hitting the shed window. Surprised to see that it wasn't Mole digging but the family from the house, he went outside to take a closer look.

'What are they doing, Robin?' Miniphant whispered.

'They are planting seeds,' Robin chirped.

'Why?' Miniphant asked.

'Because they want to grow some food.'

'Ooh! I like food,' said Miniphant, before trumping out of both ends. 'What kind of food? Ooopsie-poopsie-pardon!' he tooted excitedly.

'Vegetables,' replied Robin. 'Carrots, cauliflower, beans and tomatoes.'

Miniphant wasn't keen on vegetables. However, he noticed how **VERY** happy the family looked as they watered the seeds that were hiding in the ground.

'You must water the seeds to help them grow,' Robin sang. 'They need sunshine and good soil too,' he added as he hopped along the planted rows, amazed at the family's hard work.

Miniphant listened as the family laughed and shared what they had done together. 'They sound joyful,' Miniphant thought. 'I would like to feel like that.'

Miniphant went back into the shed. 'Feeling joyful looks lovely. I'm going to grow some food too,' he decided.

Can you guess what Miniphant wanted to grow?

Yes, baked beans and spaghetti, of course!

Not having grown anything before, he copied what he saw the family do. He emptied his suitcase and filled it with soil. Then he put beans and curled-up pieces of spaghetti in rows. After covering them up with more dirt and remembering to water them, he pushed the suitcase near the window so it would get lots of light.

Miniphant was very pleased with his efforts.

A week later, the garden vegetable patch began to show tiny little rows of green leaves – unlike Miniphant's patch, which began to show all sorts of leaves growing higgledy-piggledy-wiggledy-jiggledy all over the place inside his suitcase.

Miniphant, not knowing what baked bean plants and spaghetti trees should look like, carried on watering, and watching them grow.

After weeks of comparing his suitcase patch to the garden vegetable patch...

... Miniphant began to get a horrid feeling in his heart.

The family had grown neat rows of perfect bright green plants. But his suitcase was a crazy mixture of different types of plants – and not in neat rows at all!

His thoughts were becoming unkind and selfish.
Miniphant was starting to feel jealous.

He wanted perfect bright green plants too!

'Have the family's vegetables been watered today?' Robin asked Miniphant. The vegetables had **not** been watered, but without thinking, Miniphant lied, **'Yes, I did it this morning.'**

As soon as he'd said it, **he felt sick**. He **never** usually lied but his jealous feelings were leading to some unhelpful actions.

'Why did I say that?' he said to himself, feeling horrid inside again. He knew that lying was **not** the right thing to do, but he didn't understand why the family's vegetables were growing so nicely. Maybe by not watering theirs, his plants would grow bigger and better.

Later, Robin flew up to the shed window and saw Miniphant staring at his suitcase.

He tapped on the glass.

'Can I come in?' he chirped loudly.

Miniphant looked up and panicked. He didn't want Robin to see his suitcase patch because he was embarrassed. 'No! I'll come down to you,' he said.

Meeting him at the shed door, Robin asked, 'What's wrong, Miniphant?'

Tired of pretending everything was OK, Miniphant explained that he had been trying to grow some food like the family, but his patch didn't look **anything** like theirs.

Robin could see that Miniphant had become jealous by <u>comparing</u> the two patches instead of <u>sharing</u> the family's joy that their vegetables **were** growing wonderfully well.

'I just wanted to feel joyful too. Instead I just feel horrible,' Miniphant added honestly.

'What are you trying to grow?' Robin asked gently.

Miniphant trumped out of both ends. 'Oopsie-poopsie-pardon! My favourite foods, baked beans and lots of spaghetti!' he replied, suddenly aware of the joy he felt saying it.

Robin, being Robin, asked another question: 'And what made you think baked beans and spaghetti could be grown?'

'Well, the family are growing beans so I thought I could too, and spaghetti grows on trees, doesn't it?' Miniphant answered, imagining how that would look.

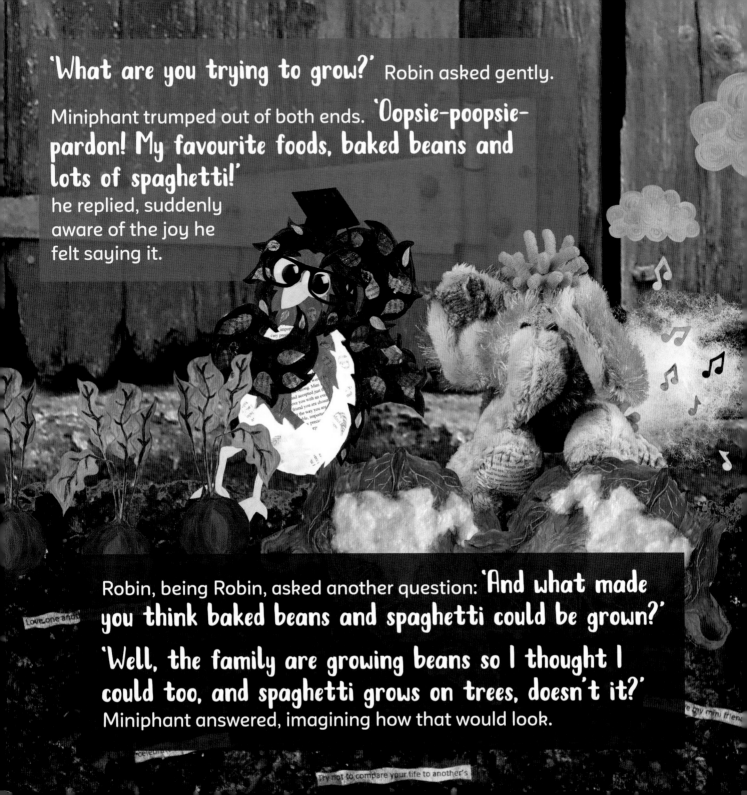

'Not everything is grown in soil, Miniphant,' Robin explained.
I can see you have done your best to grow some food,
and you have a wonderful imagination, but all you are
actually growing in your suitcase is weeds — and maybe
other weed-like feelings in your heart too,' he added softly.

WEEEEDS!!

Miniphant trumped loudly out of both ends.

'Yes, Miniphant,' replied Robin.

Miniphant felt horrid again, like there was a black scribble in his head reminding him of his jealous actions. He needed to share the truth.

'Robin?'

'Yes, Miniphant,' Robin encouraged.

'I lied when I said I had watered the family's vegetables. I didn't want theirs to grow any bigger. I'm sorry,' Miniphant whispered.

'Well done for telling the truth, Miniphant. Can you see that you are jealous of their perfect plants?' Robin went on. 'Feeling jealous has not only hurt the vegetables, it's hurt you too. Comparing has grown weeds of jealousy in your head and heart,' he explained. 'It's not easy, Miniphant, but you don't have to stay feeling jealous. Try sharing in another person's happiness, and grow seeds of joy inside you instead.'

Miniphant nodded. He did some of his best thinking and decided to make a <u>good</u> choice.

'Will you help me water the vegetable patch now, Robin? Maybe doing that will begin to turn my heart weeds into some joy-filled seeds.'

'I think that's a very good place to start, Miniphant,' Robin agreed.

Together, Robin and Miniphant began to water. Miniphant used his trunk like a hosepipe. He squirted so hard he trumped out of both ends.

'Oopsie-poopsie-pardon!' he laughed, turning the spray into a jet wash, which made him feel joyful.

Before long, the vegetables looked bigger and tastier than ever! Soon it was time to gather them up. Cat lay in the sun, watching as Miniphant emptied his suitcase of dirt and weeds. He then wrote inside the lid the lessons he'd learnt, before offering to help collect everything in it.

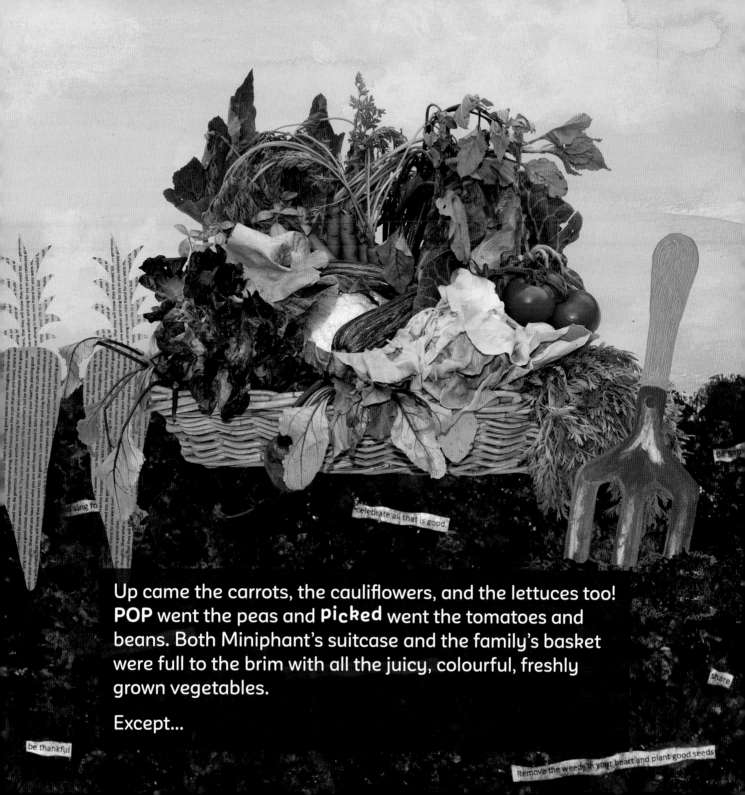

Up came the carrots, the cauliflowers, and the lettuces too! **POP** went the peas and **picked** went the tomatoes and beans. Both Miniphant's suitcase and the family's basket were full to the brim with all the juicy, colourful, freshly grown vegetables.

Except...

... one carrot got left behind.

'Oh, they missed one,' Cat meowed.

Robin hopped over to pull it up, but it wouldn't move.

Miniphant tried, but it wouldn't move.

Cat even tried to dig it out with her paws, but it still wouldn't move.

'Maybe Mole can help,' said Miniphant, before sticking his head down Mole's hill. Immediately, he saw why the carrot wouldn't move.

Mole was pulling the carrot in the opposite direction.

'We are all trying to do the same thing. Let's use our skills and share the carrot,' Miniphant trumpeted.

So the friends worked together. The animals overground pulled, while underground Mole pushed, until... **POP!** Out came the carrot, followed by Mole.

Turning the suitcase into a picnic table, the four friends celebrated the joy of growing vegetables by sharing the tasty fresh carrot, along with their own favorite food.

Miniphant tucked into a plateful of carrots and beans.
'Orange food is the best!' he said, trumping...
out of both ends!

Bedtime Thoughts and Daytime Fun

Hello again, Mini Friend!
I hope you enjoyed the story. Did you find all the carrots?
Here are some more things we can do together.

Bedtime Thoughts

Grown-ups: you can use these thinking, whispering and listening activities as part of the bedtime routine, enhancing your child's emotional literacy, mental health, and spiritual wellbeing. They are designed to be calming and settling, thought provoking, and comforting at the end of the day.

Emotional Literacy

To talk about

Jealousy is a feeling someone gets when they want something that another person has, like a toy, a skill or a special friendship. It can make us believe the lie that, without that thing, we are not good enough.

Robin told Miniphant that jealous feelings are like weeds. Weeds look ugly and horrible, and try to stop other plants from growing strong. In the same way, jealousy can feel horrible inside, look ugly outside and stop us from being joyful. It might feel like a black scribble in your head that won't go away, and you might feel a bit angry too. Outside, you might make an unhappy face by frowning, staring, stamping your feet or pressing your lips together tightly. Let's learn how we can stop jealousy quickly growing in our hearts.

Joy is a feeling of *great* happiness. Joy helps us think positively, be willing to **share** and feel thankful inside. Joy helps us to grow strong inside. Jealousy stops joy growing because it doesn't want us to feel this strong; it wants us to **compare** ourselves with others.

When we understand how jealousy works, we can try to remove it from our hearts and grow joy instead. How? By celebrating others' good news, having a party, doing a dance, telling others when good things happen to us and to people we know. When we start **sharing** in celebrating, we begin to smile, laugh and want to do kind things. It isn't always *easy*, but we can *choose* to be joyful. Even when we are going through something hard or sad, we can still look for reasons to be joyful. Why? Because joy gives us strength, which is just what we need in difficult times.

To do

Talk together about which feeling is growing stronger in your heart – is it jealousy or joy? Being honest is a good start. Why not try looking for reasons to be joyful? Practise bringing joy to those around you and grow a heart **full** of joy.

Mental Health

To talk about

Thoughts can be like seeds or weeds growing in our heads. Helpful, kind and positive thoughts or seeds can stop jealous, selfish and unhelpful weed-like thoughts from growing in our minds. This isn't easy; just like growing vegetables, it takes hard work. We need to keep checking that our thoughts are positive and kind.

To do

Has something happened this week that has grown a horrible weed thought in your head? Tell your grown-up about it. Can you and your grown-up think of a joy-filled seed thought to replace it with? Every now and then, for as long as you need to, keep thinking about your new thought so that it grows big and strong inside your head.

For example, a horrible weed thought might be: 'She's not playing with him and having *my* toy, she's *my* friend and I want that back!'

A joy-filled seed thought to replace it might be: 'Wow! I'm so thankful that I have lots of toys, and friends to share them all with.'

(Adult: This example removes any insecurity caused by jealousy a child might feel by reminding them that they have more than enough to share – toys as well as friends. The child is reassured that the friends and toys are still theirs but can be shared.)

Spiritual Wellbeing

To talk about

Miniphant's friend, Jesus, knows how *good* sharing is for us. The Bible tells us that Jesus came to help us, because we all mess up sometimes. This is good news for everyone.

If we say sorry to Jesus for our unhelpful thoughts (like comparing), our unkind feelings (like jealousy) and our messed up actions (like lying), then He will forgive us and help us to make better choices. Jesus loves us more than we can imagine.

One day, we will be able to celebrate with Jesus at the best party ever. Until then, we can all be friends with Him if we want to. Miniphant says that Jesus is the **best** friend that everyone can share! We may not be able to see Him but we choose to believe He's ready and waiting to share life with us.

To do

If you would like to ask Jesus to be your friend, you might like to say this:

Hello Jesus, thank You that You always want to be my friend. I would like to be Your forever friend too. I am sorry for all the times I have messed up. Please forgive me. Thank You for loving me so much that You want to save me and help me to make better choices. I can't wait to celebrate with You one day all the adventures that You and I are going to share together.

If you chose to say this prayer, then that's something worth celebrating and sharing with others too because it really is **good news**.

Daytime Fun

Grown-ups: these activities are designed to be interactive, fun and creative and can be integrated into your child's day to enhance their social awareness, physical wellbeing and creative thinking.

Creative Activity: Sing a Song of Joy

Did you know that, if we choose to, there are ways that can help us feel joyful? Miniphant finds that singing helps him feel joyful.

Why not make up your own song to your favourite tune using all the words you feel when you are full of joy. Often, if you sing a happy song, you will start to feel happier!

For example, when Miniphant feels joyful, he shows it by smiling, giggling, bouncing up and down and trumping out of both ends. It's a bubbly feeling inside of excitement, thankfulness and happiness rolled into one. The feeling of joyfulness comes to Miniphant when he's eating beans, going on adventures, playing with his friends, being tickled, it's someone's birthday, a friend has won a courage medal, he's made a surprise, he sees balloons and hears laughter. These are all things that Miniphant might write a song about. What would you put in your joyful song?

Practise singing your song when you need to think joyful thoughts. You can also practise **sharing** by sending the words to your song to Miniphant so he can sing it with you too (see back of book for more details on how to do that).

Social Activity: Sharing a Picnic

Sharing what you have with others is a way of showing kindness, love and generosity; this is what we call hospitality. Inviting someone to eat with you, especially if it is food you've grown or made yourself, is a great way to show hospitality.

Why not invite your friends, family or a neighbour for a picnic in a garden, at a park, in the woods or even on your living room floor. Ask everyone to bring some food or drink to share with each other. Enjoy time together, preparing the food, and laying it out on a tablecloth or blanket, like Miniphant and his friends did. What is your favourite picnic food? And who would you invite?

Physical Activity: Grow Your Own Plant

A great activity to do is grow your own plant. You don't need a garden to grow something – a small pot or even an empty eggshell can be the perfect start to growing your own food. There is nothing better than planting and caring for something, and then watching it grow before your very eyes. Physically learning how something grows, and what it needs in order to grow well, helps us to understand more about how life works.

The easiest thing you could start growing is some cress. Cress is a salad vegetable that can be eaten, or makes great hair when grown in an empty eggshell; you can then draw a funny face on the outside of the shell. Why not have a go at growing your own...

What you will need: an empty eggshell, cotton wool or tissue, cress seeds, water, pens and, if you have them, goggly eyes.

1) Take the clean empty eggshell and put some cotton wool or tissue inside it, add a little water so it becomes wet but not soggy.
2) Sprinkle some cress seeds on the top.
3) Stick on goggly eyes and draw a funny face on the front of the shell – be careful not to crack it! If you don't have goggly eyes, draw your own or use some circle stickers.
4) Place your cress head in a position where it can get some daylight.
5) Every day, see how the cress begins to grow and make sure that the cotton wool/tissue stays wet.
6) After a week or so, the seeds should have stalks with green leaves, giving your funny eggshell face some crazy hair!
7) You can either cut the hair and eat it, or let it carry on growing like hair!

Have fun! You could also have a go at growing a bean or sunflower seed in a pot of soil or in the garden, if you have one. Draw some pictures or take photos to keep a visual diary of how your plant changed as it grew!

Physical Activity: 'How I Grow' Diary

Our bodies grow too! We get bigger and stronger because we eat, drink, sleep and do different activities during the day. Why not keep a diary of how you grow too? You could draw pictures of what you have to eat; what time you go to bed to sleep and when you wake up again; what activities you did during the day to keep healthy and active; and all the other ways you look after yourself to help you grow healthy and strong (eg clean teeth, have a bath, brush hair). Keeping a diary of how you care for yourself will teach you to help care for others too.

For 'Grow Your Own Plant' and 'How I Grow' diary templates, head over to Miniphant's webpage at **cwr.org.uk/miniphant**.

Well, it's time to say goodbye, Mini Friend. I hope you have enjoyed my story! I love sharing them with you. Come and join me and my friends for more adventures in our other books.

See you **oopsie-poopsie** soon!
Love,

Miniphant x

Join Miniphant and friends for more adventures!

Miniphant & Me
Miniphant Moves In

Explores: Identity and self-worth

Miniphant & Me
One Big Adventure

Explores: Courage

Miniphant & Me
The Magnificent Raspberry Mountain

Explores: Managing anger

Miniphant & Me
Miniphant to the Rescue

Explores: Responding to change

For more information about the **Miniphant & Me** series,
including Animal Friend Fact Files, thoughts from the Bible and lots more, visit

cwr.org.uk/miniphant